Beauty

and

The Beast

Jeanne-Marie
Le Prince de Beaumont

BEAUTY AND THE BEAST

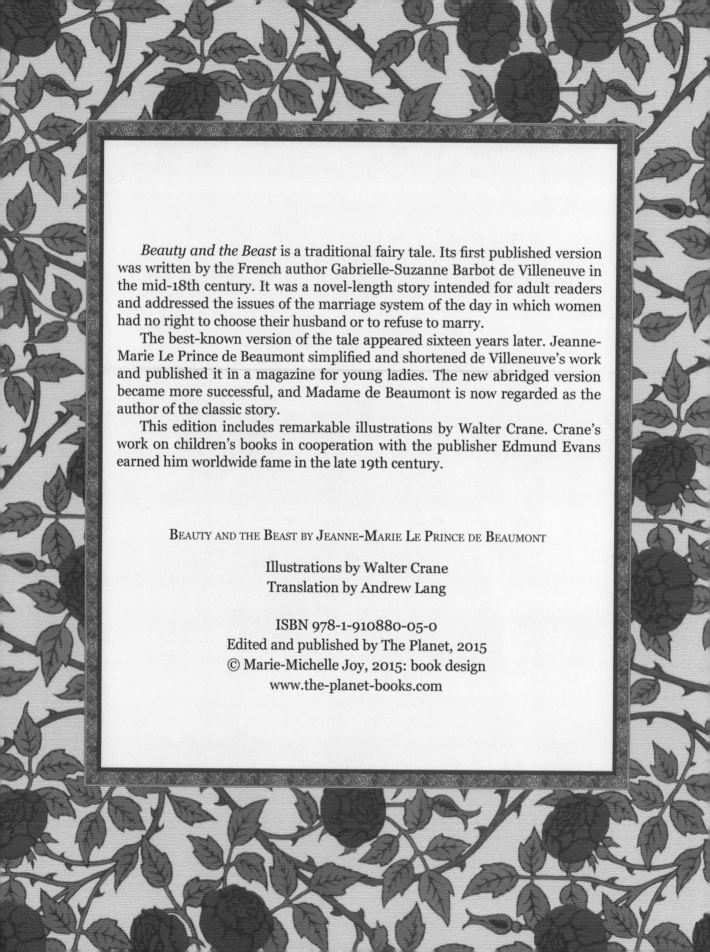

Beauty and the Beast is a traditional fairy tale. Its first published version was written by the French author Gabrielle-Suzanne Barbot de Villeneuve in the mid-18th century. It was a novel-length story intended for adult readers and addressed the issues of the marriage system of the day in which women had no right to choose their husband or to refuse to marry.

The best-known version of the tale appeared sixteen years later. Jeanne-Marie Le Prince de Beaumont simplified and shortened de Villeneuve's work and published it in a magazine for young ladies. The new abridged version became more successful, and Madame de Beaumont is now regarded as the author of the classic story.

This edition includes remarkable illustrations by Walter Crane. Crane's work on children's books in cooperation with the publisher Edmund Evans earned him worldwide fame in the late 19th century.

BEAUTY AND THE BEAST BY JEANNE-MARIE LE PRINCE DE BEAUMONT

Illustrations by Walter Crane
Translation by Andrew Lang

ISBN 978-1-910880-05-0
Edited and published by The Planet, 2015
© Marie-Michelle Joy, 2015: book design
www.the-planet-books.com

ILLUSTRATED
BY

Walter Crane

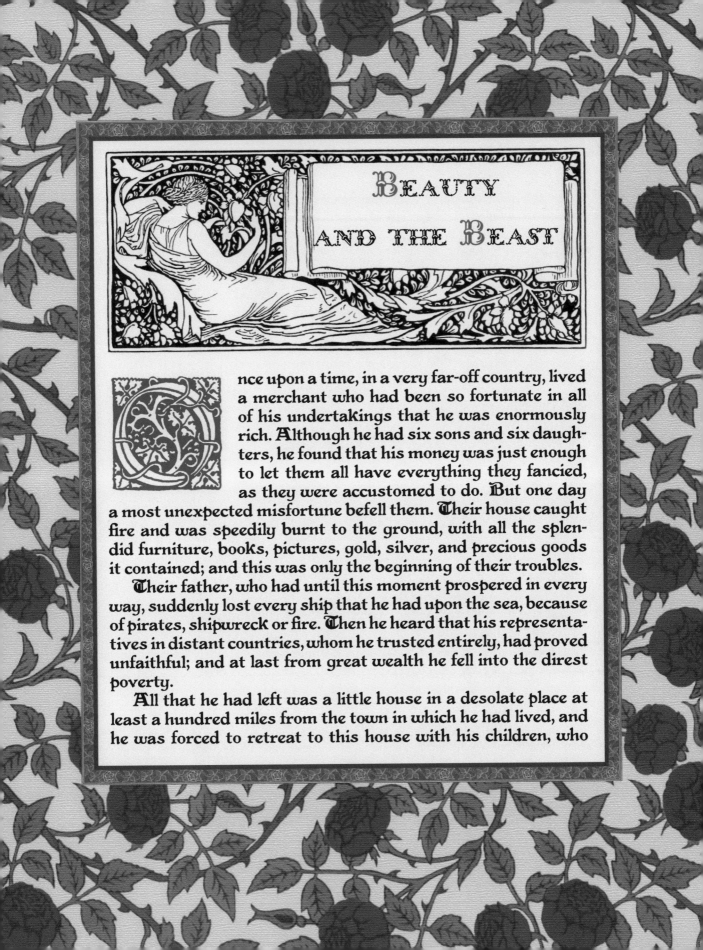

BEAUTY AND THE BEAST

nce upon a time, in a very far-off country, lived a merchant who had been so fortunate in all of his undertakings that he was enormously rich. Although he had six sons and six daughters, he found that his money was just enough to let them all have everything they fancied, as they were accustomed to do. But one day a most unexpected misfortune befell them. Their house caught fire and was speedily burnt to the ground, with all the splendid furniture, books, pictures, gold, silver, and precious goods it contained; and this was only the beginning of their troubles.

Their father, who had until this moment prospered in every way, suddenly lost every ship that he had upon the sea, because of pirates, shipwreck or fire. Then he heard that his representatives in distant countries, whom he trusted entirely, had proved unfaithful; and at last from great wealth he fell into the direst poverty.

All that he had left was a little house in a desolate place at least a hundred miles from the town in which he had lived, and he was forced to retreat to this house with his children, who

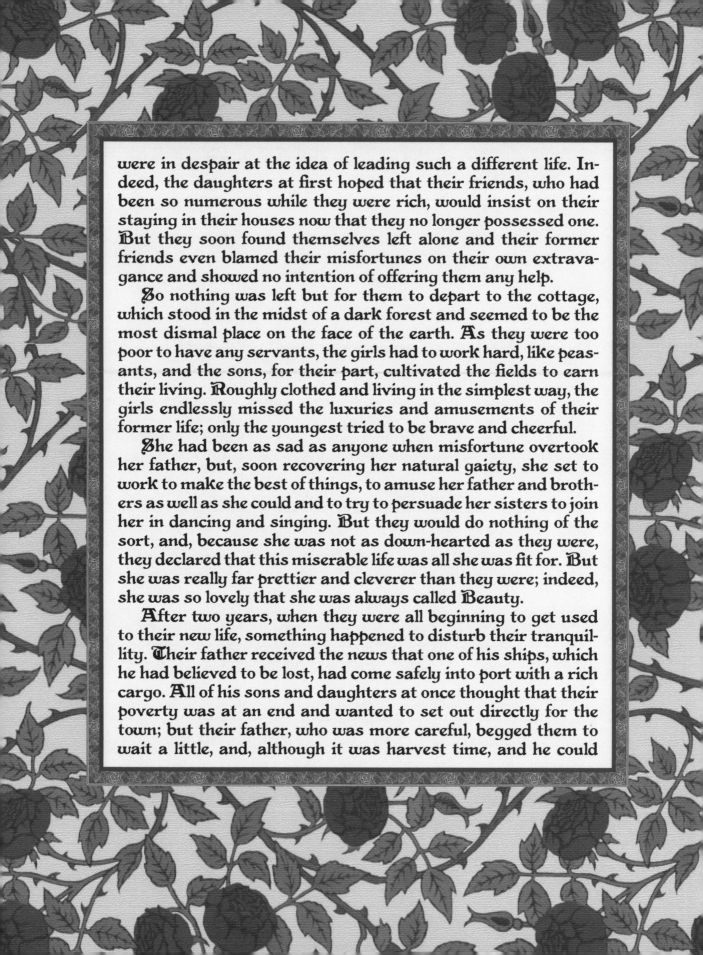

were in despair at the idea of leading such a different life. Indeed, the daughters at first hoped that their friends, who had been so numerous while they were rich, would insist on their staying in their houses now that they no longer possessed one. But they soon found themselves left alone and their former friends even blamed their misfortunes on their own extravagance and showed no intention of offering them any help.

So nothing was left but for them to depart to the cottage, which stood in the midst of a dark forest and seemed to be the most dismal place on the face of the earth. As they were too poor to have any servants, the girls had to work hard, like peasants, and the sons, for their part, cultivated the fields to earn their living. Roughly clothed and living in the simplest way, the girls endlessly missed the luxuries and amusements of their former life; only the youngest tried to be brave and cheerful.

She had been as sad as anyone when misfortune overtook her father, but, soon recovering her natural gaiety, she set to work to make the best of things, to amuse her father and brothers as well as she could and to try to persuade her sisters to join her in dancing and singing. But they would do nothing of the sort, and, because she was not as down-hearted as they were, they declared that this miserable life was all she was fit for. But she was really far prettier and cleverer than they were; indeed, she was so lovely that she was always called Beauty.

After two years, when they were all beginning to get used to their new life, something happened to disturb their tranquillity. Their father received the news that one of his ships, which he had believed to be lost, had come safely into port with a rich cargo. All of his sons and daughters at once thought that their poverty was at an end and wanted to set out directly for the town; but their father, who was more careful, begged them to wait a little, and, although it was harvest time, and he could not really be spared, determined to go himself first, to make enquiries. Only the youngest daughter had any doubt that they would soon be as rich again as they were before, or at least rich enough to live comfortably in some town where they would find amusement and jolly companions once more.

So they all loaded their father with commissions for jewels and dresses which it would have taken a fortune to buy; only Beauty, feeling sure that it was of no use, did not ask for anything. Her father, noticing her silence, said, "And what shall I bring for you, Beauty?"

"The only thing I wish for is to see you come home safely," she answered.

But this only annoyed her sisters, who imagined that she was blaming them for having asked for such costly things. Her father, however, was pleased, but as he thought that at her age she certainly ought to like pretty presents, he told her to choose something.

"Well, dear father," she said, "because you insist, I beg that you will bring me a rose. I have not seen one since we moved here, and I love them so much."

So the merchant set out and reached the town as quickly as possible, only to find that his former companions, believing him to be dead, had divided up the goods which the ship had brought between themselves; and after six months of trouble and expense, he found himself as poor as when he started, having only been able to scrape together just enough to pay for the cost of his journey. To make matters worse, he was obliged to leave the town in the most terrible weather, so that by the time he was within a few miles of his home he was almost exhausted with cold and fatigue.

Though he knew that it would take some hours to get through the forest, he was so anxious to reach the end of his

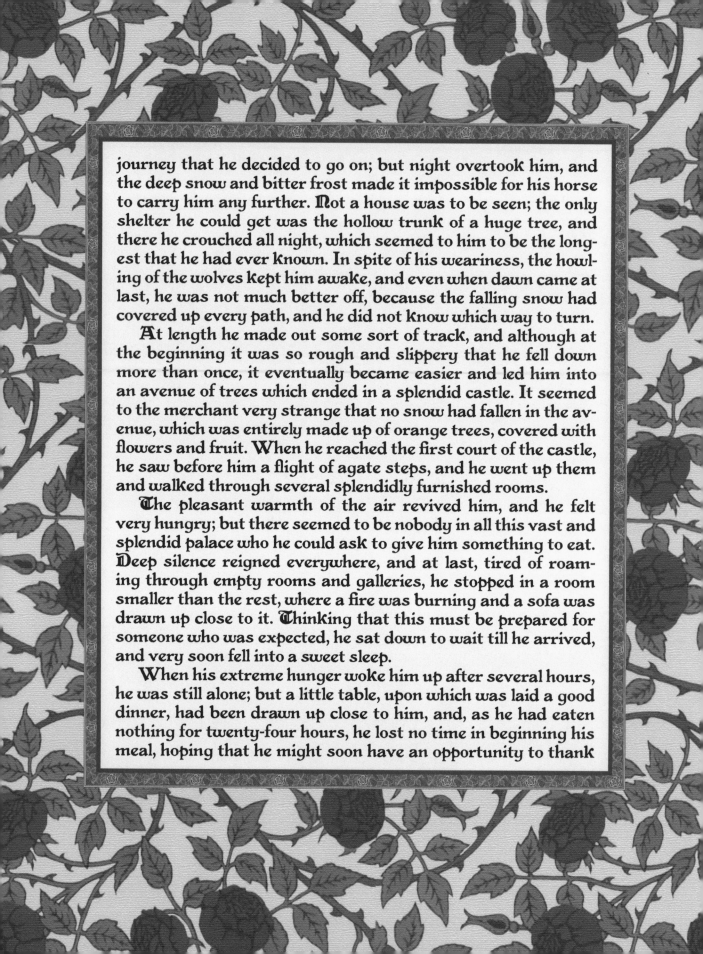

journey that he decided to go on; but night overtook him, and the deep snow and bitter frost made it impossible for his horse to carry him any further. Not a house was to be seen; the only shelter he could get was the hollow trunk of a huge tree, and there he crouched all night, which seemed to him to be the longest that he had ever known. In spite of his weariness, the howling of the wolves kept him awake, and even when dawn came at last, he was not much better off, because the falling snow had covered up every path, and he did not know which way to turn.

At length he made out some sort of track, and although at the beginning it was so rough and slippery that he fell down more than once, it eventually became easier and led him into an avenue of trees which ended in a splendid castle. It seemed to the merchant very strange that no snow had fallen in the avenue, which was entirely made up of orange trees, covered with flowers and fruit. When he reached the first court of the castle, he saw before him a flight of agate steps, and he went up them and walked through several splendidly furnished rooms.

The pleasant warmth of the air revived him, and he felt very hungry; but there seemed to be nobody in all this vast and splendid palace who he could ask to give him something to eat. Deep silence reigned everywhere, and at last, tired of roaming through empty rooms and galleries, he stopped in a room smaller than the rest, where a fire was burning and a sofa was drawn up close to it. Thinking that this must be prepared for someone who was expected, he sat down to wait till he arrived, and very soon fell into a sweet sleep.

When his extreme hunger woke him up after several hours, he was still alone; but a little table, upon which was laid a good dinner, had been drawn up close to him, and, as he had eaten nothing for twenty-four hours, he lost no time in beginning his meal, hoping that he might soon have an opportunity to thank his considerate host, whoever they might be. But no one appeared, and even after another long sleep, from which he awoke completely refreshed, there was no sign of anybody, although a fresh meal of dainty cakes and fruit had been left upon the little table at his elbow.

Being naturally timid, the silence began to terrify him, and he resolved to search once more through all the rooms; but it was of no use. Not even a servant was to be seen; there was no sign of life in the palace! He began to wonder what he should do and to amuse himself by pretending that all the treasures he saw were his own and considering how he would divide them among his children. Then he went down into the garden, and although it was winter everywhere else, here the sun shone, and the birds sang, and the flowers bloomed, and the air was soft and sweet.

The merchant, thrilled with everything he saw and heard, said to himself, "All of this must be meant for me. I will go home this minute and bring my children to share all these delights."

In spite of being so cold and weary when he reached the castle, he had taken his horse to the stable and fed it. Now he thought he would saddle it for his homeward journey, and he turned down the path which led to the stable. This path had a hedge of roses on each side of it, and the merchant thought that he had never seen or smelt such exquisite flowers.

They reminded him of his promise to Beauty, and he stopped and had just picked one to take to her when he was startled by a strange noise behind him. Turning round, he saw a frightful Beast, which seemed to be very angry, and said in a terrible voice, "Who told you that you could pick my roses? Was it not enough that I allowed you to be in my palace and was kind to you? This is the way you show your gratitude: by stealing my flowers! But your insolence shall not go unpunished."

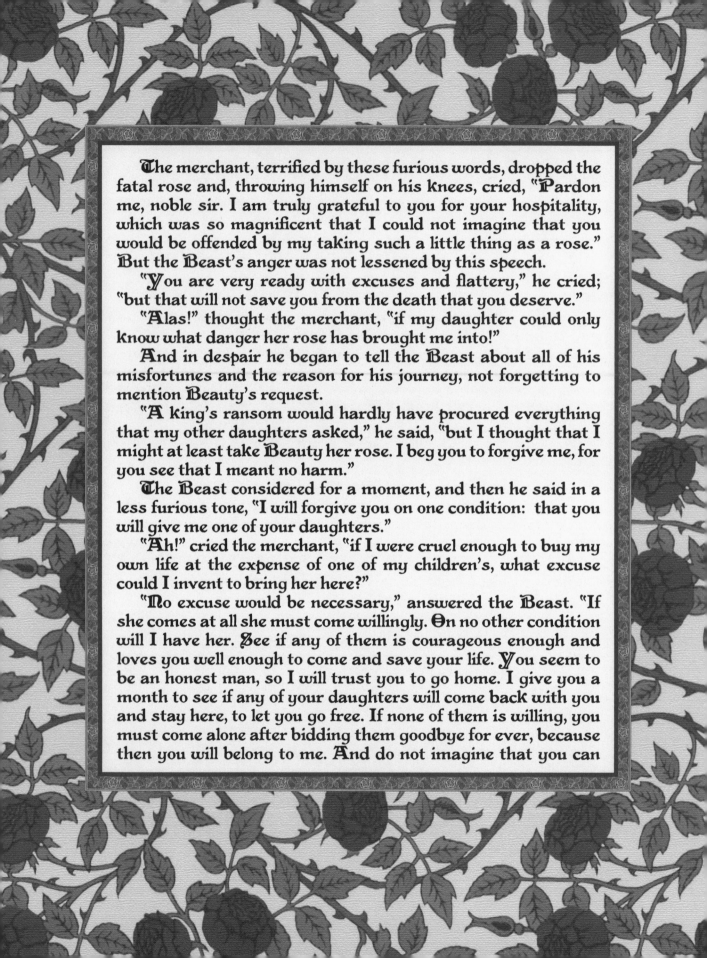

The merchant, terrified by these furious words, dropped the fatal rose and, throwing himself on his knees, cried, "Pardon me, noble sir. I am truly grateful to you for your hospitality, which was so magnificent that I could not imagine that you would be offended by my taking such a little thing as a rose." But the Beast's anger was not lessened by this speech.

"You are very ready with excuses and flattery," he cried; "but that will not save you from the death that you deserve."

"Alas!" thought the merchant, "if my daughter could only know what danger her rose has brought me into!"

And in despair he began to tell the Beast about all of his misfortunes and the reason for his journey, not forgetting to mention Beauty's request.

"A king's ransom would hardly have procured everything that my other daughters asked," he said, "but I thought that I might at least take Beauty her rose. I beg you to forgive me, for you see that I meant no harm."

The Beast considered for a moment, and then he said in a less furious tone, "I will forgive you on one condition: that you will give me one of your daughters."

"Ah!" cried the merchant, "if I were cruel enough to buy my own life at the expense of one of my children's, what excuse could I invent to bring her here?"

"No excuse would be necessary," answered the Beast. "If she comes at all she must come willingly. On no other condition will I have her. See if any of them is courageous enough and loves you well enough to come and save your life. You seem to be an honest man, so I will trust you to go home. I give you a month to see if any of your daughters will come back with you and stay here, to let you go free. If none of them is willing, you must come alone after bidding them goodbye for ever, because then you will belong to me. And do not imagine that you can

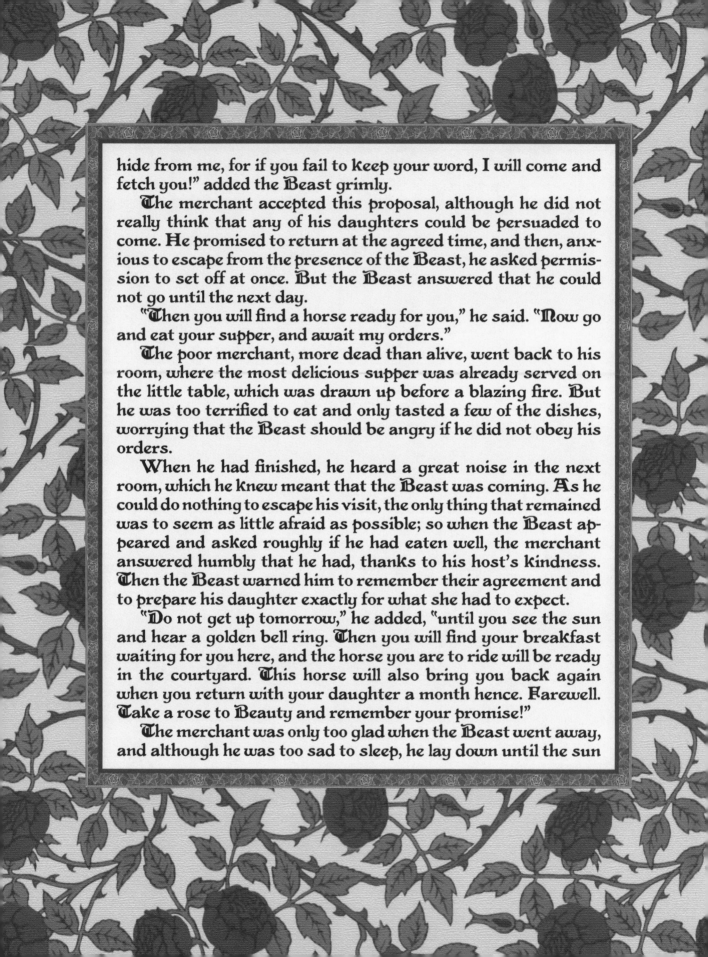

hide from me, for if you fail to keep your word, I will come and fetch you!" added the Beast grimly.

The merchant accepted this proposal, although he did not really think that any of his daughters could be persuaded to come. He promised to return at the agreed time, and then, anxious to escape from the presence of the Beast, he asked permission to set off at once. But the Beast answered that he could not go until the next day.

"Then you will find a horse ready for you," he said. "Now go and eat your supper, and await my orders."

The poor merchant, more dead than alive, went back to his room, where the most delicious supper was already served on the little table, which was drawn up before a blazing fire. But he was too terrified to eat and only tasted a few of the dishes, worrying that the Beast should be angry if he did not obey his orders.

When he had finished, he heard a great noise in the next room, which he knew meant that the Beast was coming. As he could do nothing to escape his visit, the only thing that remained was to seem as little afraid as possible; so when the Beast appeared and asked roughly if he had eaten well, the merchant answered humbly that he had, thanks to his host's kindness. Then the Beast warned him to remember their agreement and to prepare his daughter exactly for what she had to expect.

"Do not get up tomorrow," he added, "until you see the sun and hear a golden bell ring. Then you will find your breakfast waiting for you here, and the horse you are to ride will be ready in the courtyard. This horse will also bring you back again when you return with your daughter a month hence. Farewell. Take a rose to Beauty and remember your promise!"

The merchant was only too glad when the Beast went away, and although he was too sad to sleep, he lay down until the sun

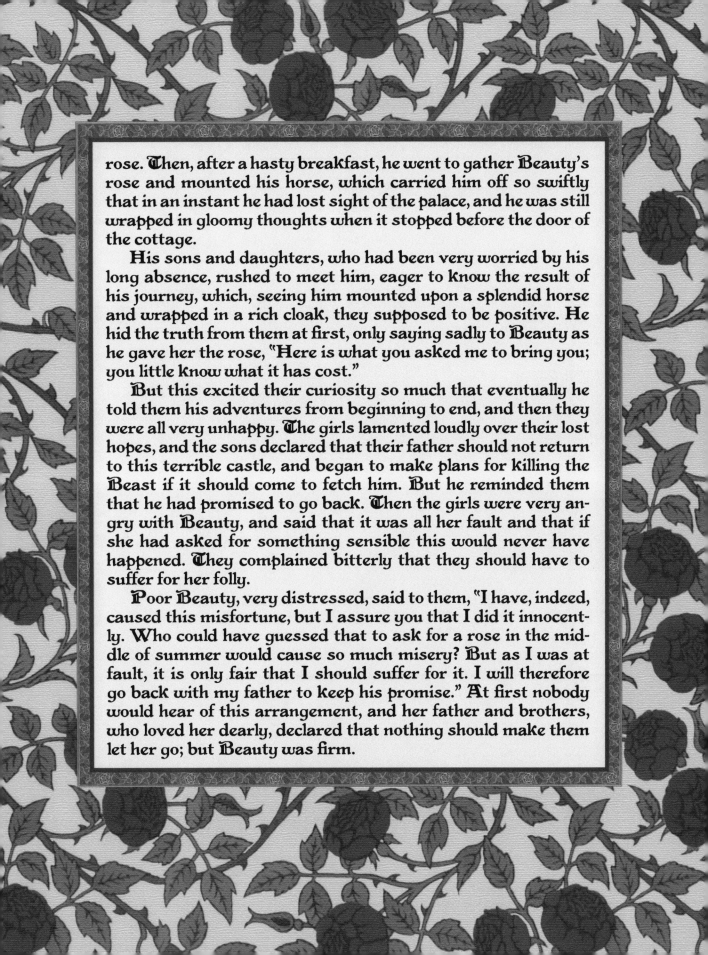

rose. Then, after a hasty breakfast, he went to gather Beauty's rose and mounted his horse, which carried him off so swiftly that in an instant he had lost sight of the palace, and he was still wrapped in gloomy thoughts when it stopped before the door of the cottage.

His sons and daughters, who had been very worried by his long absence, rushed to meet him, eager to know the result of his journey, which, seeing him mounted upon a splendid horse and wrapped in a rich cloak, they supposed to be positive. He hid the truth from them at first, only saying sadly to Beauty as he gave her the rose, "Here is what you asked me to bring you; you little know what it has cost."

But this excited their curiosity so much that eventually he told them his adventures from beginning to end, and then they were all very unhappy. The girls lamented loudly over their lost hopes, and the sons declared that their father should not return to this terrible castle, and began to make plans for killing the Beast if it should come to fetch him. But he reminded them that he had promised to go back. Then the girls were very angry with Beauty, and said that it was all her fault and that if she had asked for something sensible this would never have happened. They complained bitterly that they should have to suffer for her folly.

Poor Beauty, very distressed, said to them, "I have, indeed, caused this misfortune, but I assure you that I did it innocently. Who could have guessed that to ask for a rose in the middle of summer would cause so much misery? But as I was at fault, it is only fair that I should suffer for it. I will therefore go back with my father to keep his promise." At first nobody would hear of this arrangement, and her father and brothers, who loved her dearly, declared that nothing should make them let her go; but Beauty was firm.

As the time drew near, she divided all of her few possessions between her sisters and said goodbye to everything she loved; and when the fatal day came, she encouraged and cheered her father as they mounted together the horse which had brought him back. It seemed to fly rather than gallop, but so smoothly that Beauty was not frightened; indeed, she would have enjoyed the journey if she had not been afraid of what might happen to her at the end of it. Her father still tried to persuade her to go back, but it was no use.

While they were talking, the night fell, and then, to their great surprise, wonderful coloured lights began to shine in all directions, and splendid fireworks blazed out before them; all of the forest was illuminated by them, and even felt pleasantly warm, although it had been bitterly cold before. This lasted until they reached the avenue of orange trees, where were statues holding flaming torches; and when they got nearer to the palace, they saw that it was illuminated from the roof to the ground, and music sounded softly from the courtyard.

"The Beast must be very hungry," said Beauty, trying to laugh, "if he makes all this rejoicing over the arrival of his prey."

But, in spite of her anxiety, she could not help admiring all the wonderful things that she saw.

The horse stopped at the foot of the flight of steps leading to the terrace, and when they had dismounted, her father led her to the little room he had been in before, where they found a splendid fire burning and the table daintily spread with a delicious supper.

The merchant knew that this was meant for them, and Beauty, who was rather less frightened now that she had passed through so many rooms and seen nothing of the Beast, was quite willing to begin to eat, for her long ride had made her very hungry.

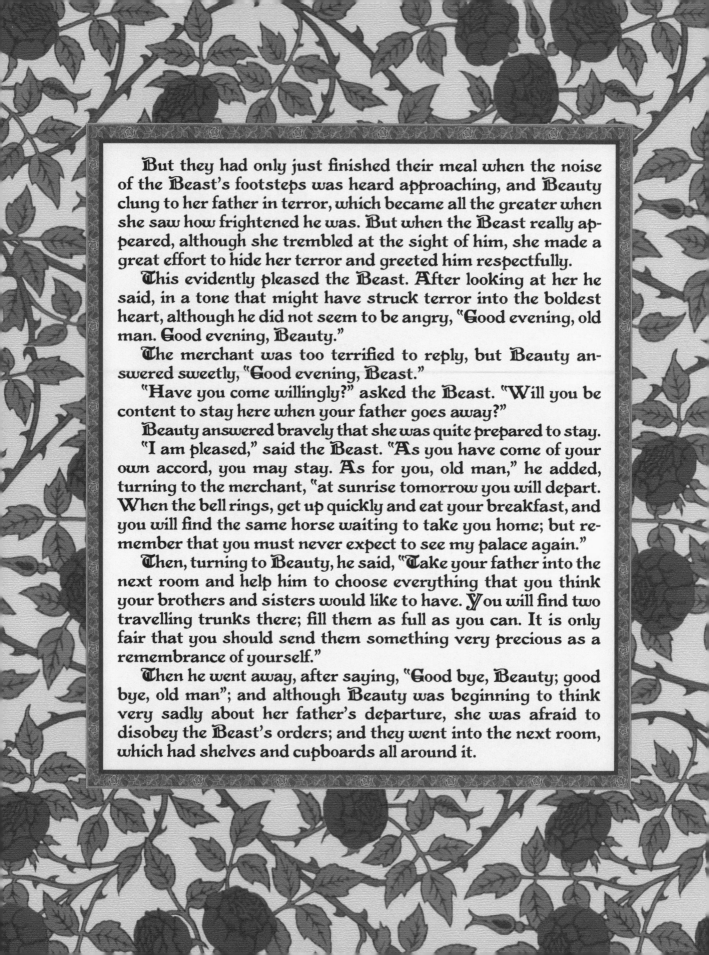

But they had only just finished their meal when the noise of the Beast's footsteps was heard approaching, and Beauty clung to her father in terror, which became all the greater when she saw how frightened he was. But when the Beast really appeared, although she trembled at the sight of him, she made a great effort to hide her terror and greeted him respectfully.

This evidently pleased the Beast. After looking at her he said, in a tone that might have struck terror into the boldest heart, although he did not seem to be angry, "Good evening, old man. Good evening, Beauty."

The merchant was too terrified to reply, but Beauty answered sweetly, "Good evening, Beast."

"Have you come willingly?" asked the Beast. "Will you be content to stay here when your father goes away?"

Beauty answered bravely that she was quite prepared to stay.

"I am pleased," said the Beast. "As you have come of your own accord, you may stay. As for you, old man," he added, turning to the merchant, "at sunrise tomorrow you will depart. When the bell rings, get up quickly and eat your breakfast, and you will find the same horse waiting to take you home; but remember that you must never expect to see my palace again."

Then, turning to Beauty, he said, "Take your father into the next room and help him to choose everything that you think your brothers and sisters would like to have. You will find two travelling trunks there; fill them as full as you can. It is only fair that you should send them something very precious as a remembrance of yourself."

Then he went away, after saying, "Good bye, Beauty; good bye, old man"; and although Beauty was beginning to think very sadly about her father's departure, she was afraid to disobey the Beast's orders; and they went into the next room, which had shelves and cupboards all around it.

They were greatly surprised at the riches it contained. There were splendid dresses fit for a queen, with all of the ornaments that were to be worn with them; and when Beauty opened the cupboards, she was quite dazzled by the gorgeous jewels that lay in heaps upon every shelf. After choosing a vast quantity, which she divided between her sisters – for she had made a heap of the wonderful dresses for each of them – she opened the last chest, which was full of gold.

"I think, father," she said, "that, as the gold will be more useful to you, we had better take the other things out again and fill the trunks with it."

So they did this; but the more they put in, the more room there seemed to be, and at last they put back all the jewels and dresses they had taken out, and Beauty even added as many more of the jewels as she could carry at once; and then the trunks were not too full, but they were so heavy that an elephant could not have carried them!

"The Beast was mocking us!" cried the merchant. "He must have pretended to give us all of these things, knowing that I could not carry them away."

"Let us wait and see," answered Beauty. "I cannot believe that he meant to deceive us. All we can do is to fasten them up and leave them ready."

So they did this and returned to the little room, where, to their astonishment, they found breakfast ready. The merchant ate his with a good appetite, as the Beast's generosity made him believe that he might perhaps dare to come back soon and see Beauty. But she felt sure that her father was leaving her forever, so she was very sad when the bell rang sharply for the second time and warned them that the time had come for them to part.

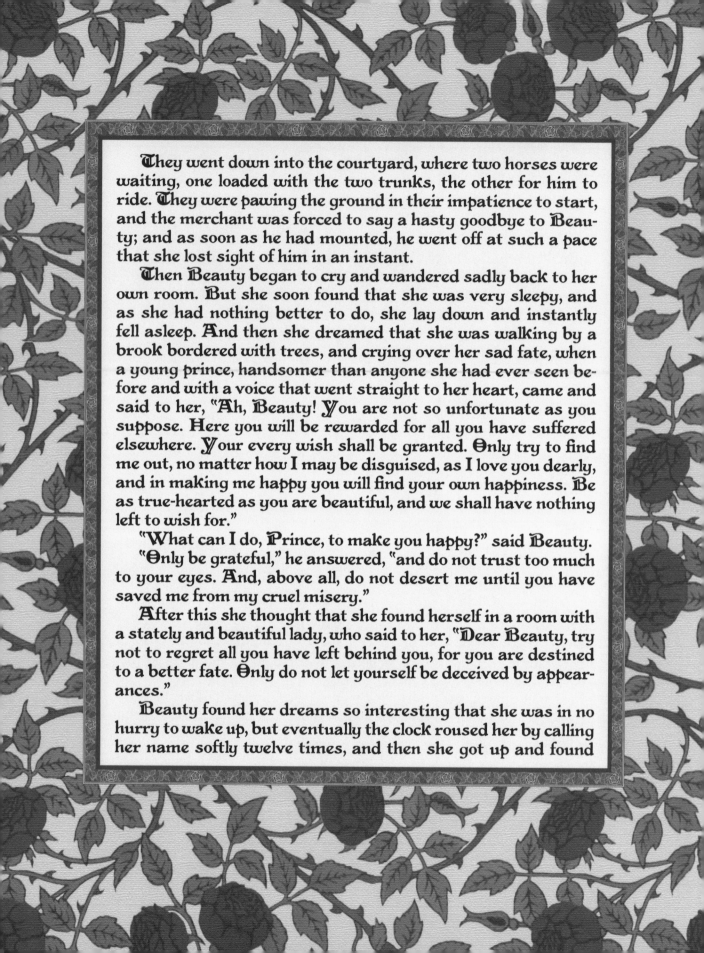

They went down into the courtyard, where two horses were waiting, one loaded with the two trunks, the other for him to ride. They were pawing the ground in their impatience to start, and the merchant was forced to say a hasty goodbye to Beauty; and as soon as he had mounted, he went off at such a pace that she lost sight of him in an instant.

Then Beauty began to cry and wandered sadly back to her own room. But she soon found that she was very sleepy, and as she had nothing better to do, she lay down and instantly fell asleep. And then she dreamed that she was walking by a brook bordered with trees, and crying over her sad fate, when a young prince, handsomer than anyone she had ever seen before and with a voice that went straight to her heart, came and said to her, "Ah, Beauty! You are not so unfortunate as you suppose. Here you will be rewarded for all you have suffered elsewhere. Your every wish shall be granted. Only try to find me out, no matter how I may be disguised, as I love you dearly, and in making me happy you will find your own happiness. Be as true-hearted as you are beautiful, and we shall have nothing left to wish for."

"What can I do, Prince, to make you happy?" said Beauty.

"Only be grateful," he answered, "and do not trust too much to your eyes. And, above all, do not desert me until you have saved me from my cruel misery."

After this she thought that she found herself in a room with a stately and beautiful lady, who said to her, "Dear Beauty, try not to regret all you have left behind you, for you are destined to a better fate. Only do not let yourself be deceived by appearances."

Beauty found her dreams so interesting that she was in no hurry to wake up, but eventually the clock roused her by calling her name softly twelve times, and then she got up and found

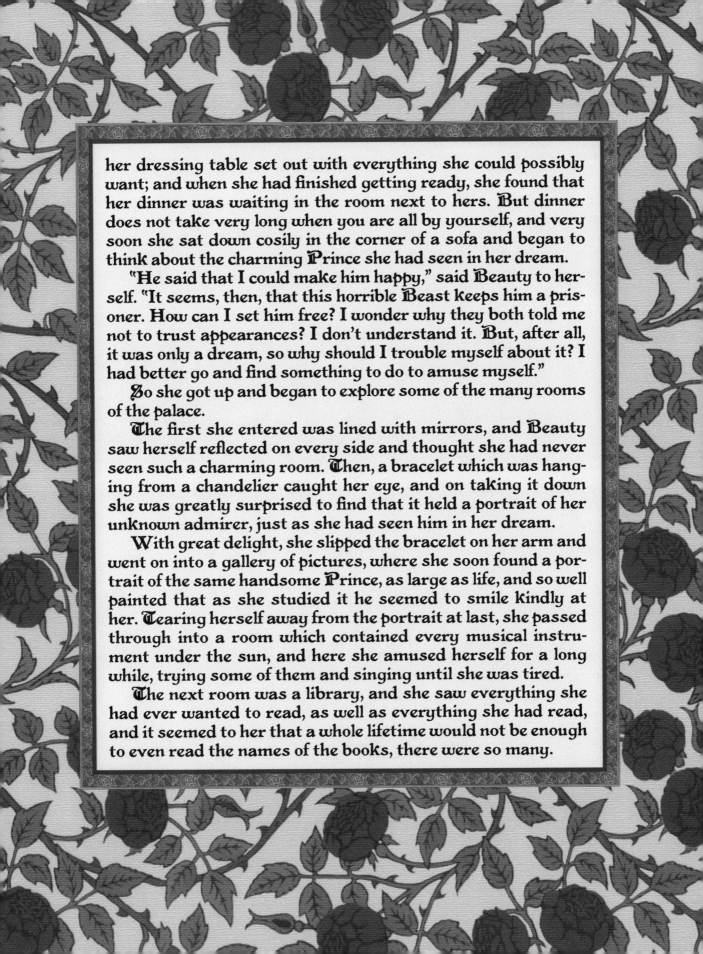

her dressing table set out with everything she could possibly want; and when she had finished getting ready, she found that her dinner was waiting in the room next to hers. But dinner does not take very long when you are all by yourself, and very soon she sat down cosily in the corner of a sofa and began to think about the charming Prince she had seen in her dream.

"He said that I could make him happy," said Beauty to herself. "It seems, then, that this horrible Beast keeps him a prisoner. How can I set him free? I wonder why they both told me not to trust appearances? I don't understand it. But, after all, it was only a dream, so why should I trouble myself about it? I had better go and find something to do to amuse myself."

So she got up and began to explore some of the many rooms of the palace.

The first she entered was lined with mirrors, and Beauty saw herself reflected on every side and thought she had never seen such a charming room. Then, a bracelet which was hanging from a chandelier caught her eye, and on taking it down she was greatly surprised to find that it held a portrait of her unknown admirer, just as she had seen him in her dream.

With great delight, she slipped the bracelet on her arm and went on into a gallery of pictures, where she soon found a portrait of the same handsome Prince, as large as life, and so well painted that as she studied it he seemed to smile kindly at her. Tearing herself away from the portrait at last, she passed through into a room which contained every musical instrument under the sun, and here she amused herself for a long while, trying some of them and singing until she was tired.

The next room was a library, and she saw everything she had ever wanted to read, as well as everything she had read, and it seemed to her that a whole lifetime would not be enough to even read the names of the books, there were so many.

By this time it was getting dark, and wax candles in diamond and ruby candlesticks were beginning to light themselves in every room.

Beauty found her supper served just at the time she liked to have it, but she did not see anyone or hear a sound, and, although her father had warned her that she would be alone, she began to find it rather dull. But eventually she heard the Beast coming and wondered tremblingly if he intended to eat her up now.

However, as he did not seem at all ferocious and only said gruffly, "Good evening, Beauty," she answered cheerfully and managed to conceal her terror. Then the Beast asked her how she had been amusing herself, and she told him about all the rooms she had seen.

Then he asked if she thought she could be happy in his palace; and Beauty answered that everything was so beautiful that she would be very hard to please if she could not be happy. After they had talked for an hour, Beauty began to think that the Beast was not nearly so terrible as she had first thought. Then he got up to leave her and said in his gruff voice, "Do you love me, Beauty? Will you marry me?"

"Oh! what shall I say?" cried Beauty, for she was afraid to make the Beast angry by refusing.

"Say 'yes' or 'no' without fear," he replied.

"Oh! no, Beast," said Beauty hastily.

"Since you will not, good night, Beauty," he said.

And she answered, "Good night, Beast," very glad to find that her refusal had not provoked him.

After he had gone, she was very soon in bed and asleep, and dreaming of her unknown Prince. She thought that he came and said to her, "Ah, Beauty! Why are you so unkind to me? I fear I am fated to be unhappy for many a long day still."

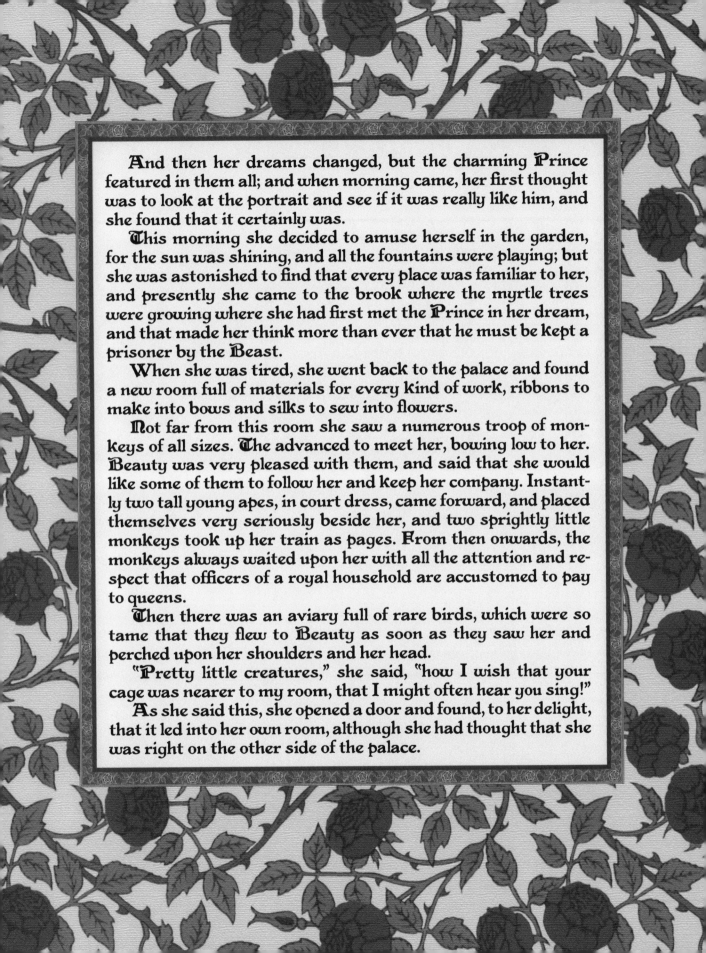

And then her dreams changed, but the charming Prince featured in them all; and when morning came, her first thought was to look at the portrait and see if it was really like him, and she found that it certainly was.

This morning she decided to amuse herself in the garden, for the sun was shining, and all the fountains were playing; but she was astonished to find that every place was familiar to her, and presently she came to the brook where the myrtle trees were growing where she had first met the Prince in her dream, and that made her think more than ever that he must be kept a prisoner by the Beast.

When she was tired, she went back to the palace and found a new room full of materials for every kind of work, ribbons to make into bows and silks to sew into flowers.

Not far from this room she saw a numerous troop of monkeys of all sizes. The advanced to meet her, bowing low to her. Beauty was very pleased with them, and said that she would like some of them to follow her and keep her company. Instantly two tall young apes, in court dress, came forward, and placed themselves very seriously beside her, and two sprightly little monkeys took up her train as pages. From then onwards, the monkeys always waited upon her with all the attention and respect that officers of a royal household are accustomed to pay to queens.

Then there was an aviary full of rare birds, which were so tame that they flew to Beauty as soon as they saw her and perched upon her shoulders and her head.

"Pretty little creatures," she said, "how I wish that your cage was nearer to my room, that I might often hear you sing!"

As she said this, she opened a door and found, to her delight, that it led into her own room, although she had thought that she was right on the other side of the palace.

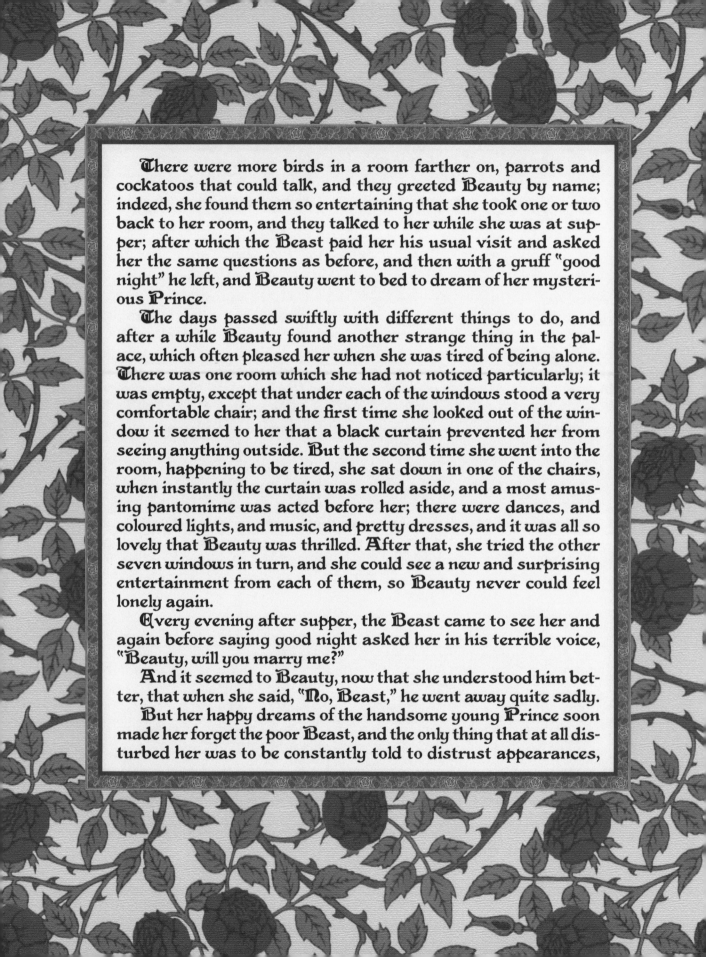

There were more birds in a room farther on, parrots and cockatoos that could talk, and they greeted Beauty by name; indeed, she found them so entertaining that she took one or two back to her room, and they talked to her while she was at supper; after which the Beast paid her his usual visit and asked her the same questions as before, and then with a gruff "good night" he left, and Beauty went to bed to dream of her mysterious Prince.

The days passed swiftly with different things to do, and after a while Beauty found another strange thing in the palace, which often pleased her when she was tired of being alone. There was one room which she had not noticed particularly; it was empty, except that under each of the windows stood a very comfortable chair; and the first time she looked out of the window it seemed to her that a black curtain prevented her from seeing anything outside. But the second time she went into the room, happening to be tired, she sat down in one of the chairs, when instantly the curtain was rolled aside, and a most amusing pantomime was acted before her; there were dances, and coloured lights, and music, and pretty dresses, and it was all so lovely that Beauty was thrilled. After that, she tried the other seven windows in turn, and she could see a new and surprising entertainment from each of them, so Beauty never could feel lonely again.

Every evening after supper, the Beast came to see her and again before saying good night asked her in his terrible voice, "Beauty, will you marry me?"

And it seemed to Beauty, now that she understood him better, that when she said, "No, Beast," he went away quite sadly.

But her happy dreams of the handsome young Prince soon made her forget the poor Beast, and the only thing that at all disturbed her was to be constantly told to distrust appearances,

to let her heart guide her, and not her eyes, and many other equally perplexing things, which she could not understand, however much she thought about them.

So everything went on for a long time, until at last, even though she was happy, Beauty began to long for the sight of her father and her brothers and sisters; and one night, seeing that she was looking very sad, the Beast asked her what was the matter.

Beauty had completely stopped being afraid of him. Now she knew that he was really gentle in spite of his ferocious looks and his dreadful voice. So she answered that she was longing to see her home once more.

When he heard this, the Beast seemed sad and distressed and cried miserably.

"Ah! Beauty, have you the heart to desert an unhappy Beast like this? What more do you want to make you happy? Is it because you hate me that you want to escape?"

"No, dear Beast," answered Beauty softly, "I do not hate you, and I should be very sorry never to see you any more, but I long to see my father again. Only let me go for two months, and I promise to come back to you and stay for the rest of my life."

The Beast, who had been sighing sadly while she spoke, now replied, "I cannot refuse you anything you ask, even if it cost me my life. Take the four boxes that you find in the room next to your own and fill them with everything that you wish to take with you. But remember your promise and come back when the two months are over, or you might regret it, for if you do not come in good time, you will find your faithful Beast dead. You will not need a carriage to bring you back. Only say good bye to all your brothers and sisters the night before you come away, and when you have gone to bed turn this ring round upon your finger and say firmly: 'I wish to go back to my palace and

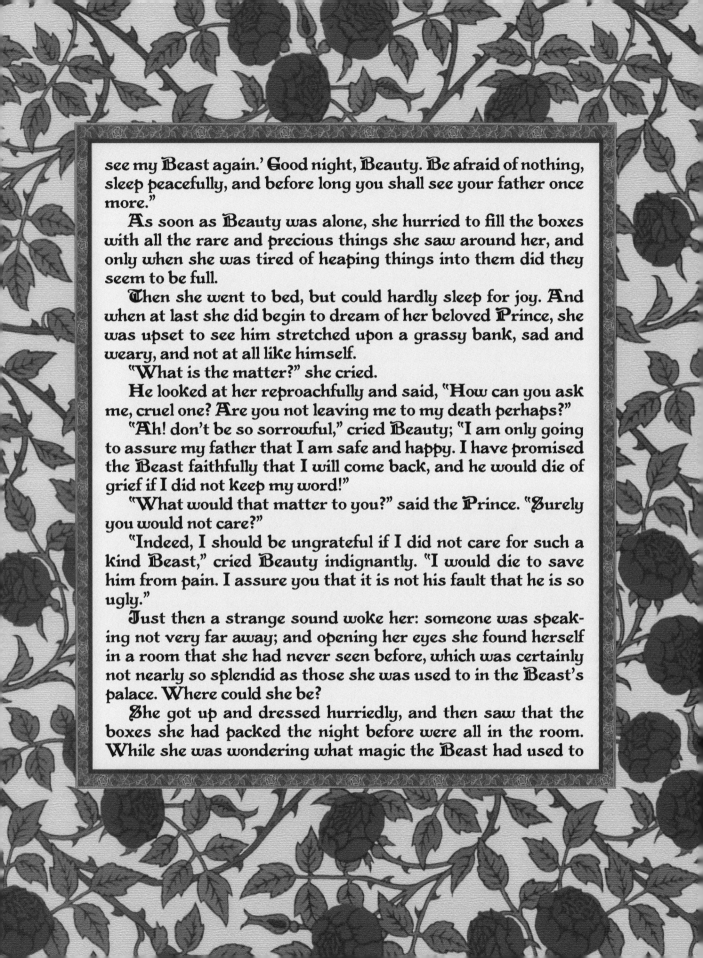

see my Beast again.' Good night, Beauty. Be afraid of nothing, sleep peacefully, and before long you shall see your father once more."

As soon as Beauty was alone, she hurried to fill the boxes with all the rare and precious things she saw around her, and only when she was tired of heaping things into them did they seem to be full.

Then she went to bed, but could hardly sleep for joy. And when at last she did begin to dream of her beloved Prince, she was upset to see him stretched upon a grassy bank, sad and weary, and not at all like himself.

"What is the matter?" she cried.

He looked at her reproachfully and said, "How can you ask me, cruel one? Are you not leaving me to my death perhaps?"

"Ah! don't be so sorrowful," cried Beauty; "I am only going to assure my father that I am safe and happy. I have promised the Beast faithfully that I will come back, and he would die of grief if I did not keep my word!"

"What would that matter to you?" said the Prince. "Surely you would not care?"

"Indeed, I should be ungrateful if I did not care for such a kind Beast," cried Beauty indignantly. "I would die to save him from pain. I assure you that it is not his fault that he is so ugly."

Just then a strange sound woke her: someone was speaking not very far away; and opening her eyes she found herself in a room that she had never seen before, which was certainly not nearly so splendid as those she was used to in the Beast's palace. Where could she be?

She got up and dressed hurriedly, and then saw that the boxes she had packed the night before were all in the room. While she was wondering what magic the Beast had used to

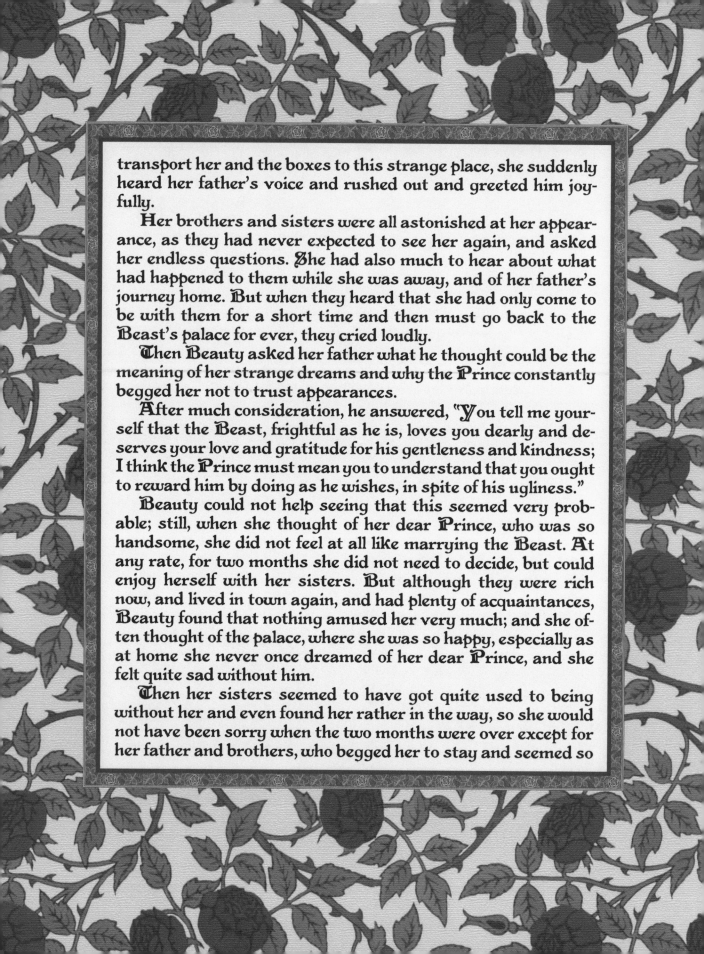

transport her and the boxes to this strange place, she suddenly heard her father's voice and rushed out and greeted him joyfully.

Her brothers and sisters were all astonished at her appearance, as they had never expected to see her again, and asked her endless questions. She had also much to hear about what had happened to them while she was away, and of her father's journey home. But when they heard that she had only come to be with them for a short time and then must go back to the Beast's palace for ever, they cried loudly.

Then Beauty asked her father what he thought could be the meaning of her strange dreams and why the Prince constantly begged her not to trust appearances.

After much consideration, he answered, "You tell me yourself that the Beast, frightful as he is, loves you dearly and deserves your love and gratitude for his gentleness and kindness; I think the Prince must mean you to understand that you ought to reward him by doing as he wishes, in spite of his ugliness."

Beauty could not help seeing that this seemed very probable; still, when she thought of her dear Prince, who was so handsome, she did not feel at all like marrying the Beast. At any rate, for two months she did not need to decide, but could enjoy herself with her sisters. But although they were rich now, and lived in town again, and had plenty of acquaintances, Beauty found that nothing amused her very much; and she often thought of the palace, where she was so happy, especially as at home she never once dreamed of her dear Prince, and she felt quite sad without him.

Then her sisters seemed to have got quite used to being without her and even found her rather in the way, so she would not have been sorry when the two months were over except for her father and brothers, who begged her to stay and seemed so

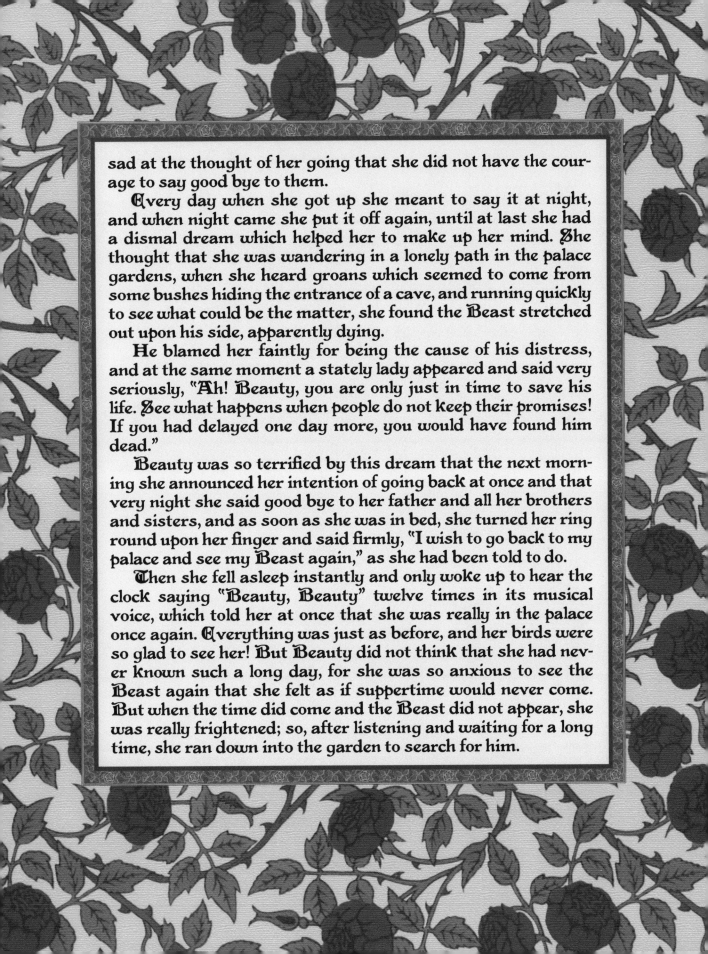

sad at the thought of her going that she did not have the courage to say good bye to them.

Every day when she got up she meant to say it at night, and when night came she put it off again, until at last she had a dismal dream which helped her to make up her mind. She thought that she was wandering in a lonely path in the palace gardens, when she heard groans which seemed to come from some bushes hiding the entrance of a cave, and running quickly to see what could be the matter, she found the Beast stretched out upon his side, apparently dying.

He blamed her faintly for being the cause of his distress, and at the same moment a stately lady appeared and said very seriously, "Ah! Beauty, you are only just in time to save his life. See what happens when people do not keep their promises! If you had delayed one day more, you would have found him dead."

Beauty was so terrified by this dream that the next morning she announced her intention of going back at once and that very night she said good bye to her father and all her brothers and sisters, and as soon as she was in bed, she turned her ring round upon her finger and said firmly, "I wish to go back to my palace and see my Beast again," as she had been told to do.

Then she fell asleep instantly and only woke up to hear the clock saying "Beauty, Beauty" twelve times in its musical voice, which told her at once that she was really in the palace once again. Everything was just as before, and her birds were so glad to see her! But Beauty did not think that she had never known such a long day, for she was so anxious to see the Beast again that she felt as if suppertime would never come. But when the time did come and the Beast did not appear, she was really frightened; so, after listening and waiting for a long time, she ran down into the garden to search for him.

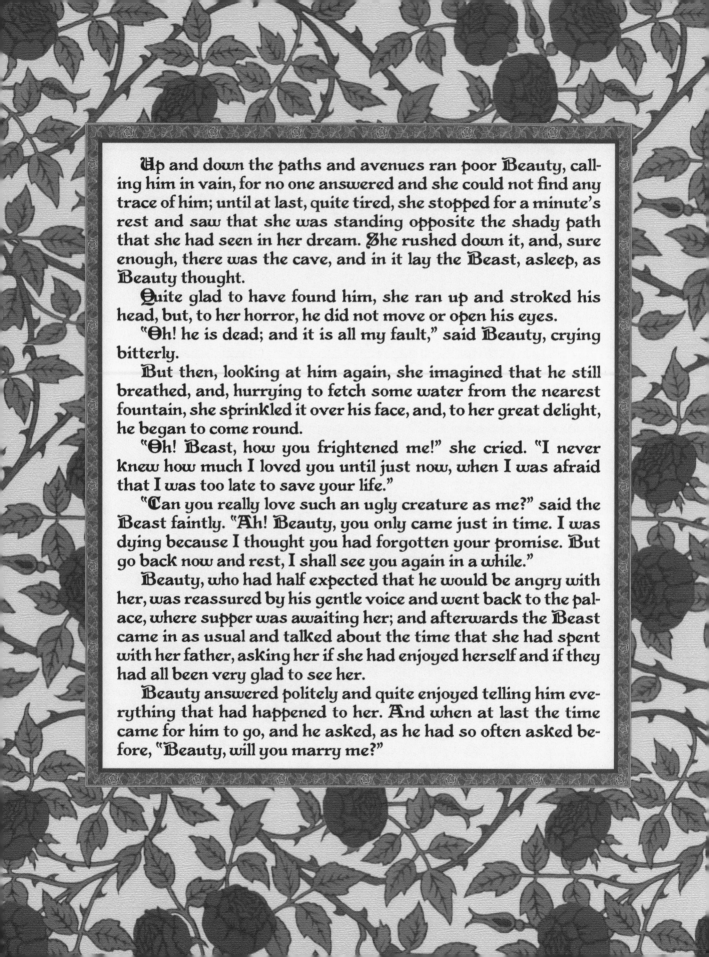

Up and down the paths and avenues ran poor Beauty, calling him in vain, for no one answered and she could not find any trace of him; until at last, quite tired, she stopped for a minute's rest and saw that she was standing opposite the shady path that she had seen in her dream. She rushed down it, and, sure enough, there was the cave, and in it lay the Beast, asleep, as Beauty thought.

Quite glad to have found him, she ran up and stroked his head, but, to her horror, he did not move or open his eyes.

"Oh! he is dead; and it is all my fault," said Beauty, crying bitterly.

But then, looking at him again, she imagined that he still breathed, and, hurrying to fetch some water from the nearest fountain, she sprinkled it over his face, and, to her great delight, he began to come round.

"Oh! Beast, how you frightened me!" she cried. "I never knew how much I loved you until just now, when I was afraid that I was too late to save your life."

"Can you really love such an ugly creature as me?" said the Beast faintly. "Ah! Beauty, you only came just in time. I was dying because I thought you had forgotten your promise. But go back now and rest, I shall see you again in a while."

Beauty, who had half expected that he would be angry with her, was reassured by his gentle voice and went back to the palace, where supper was awaiting her; and afterwards the Beast came in as usual and talked about the time that she had spent with her father, asking her if she had enjoyed herself and if they had all been very glad to see her.

Beauty answered politely and quite enjoyed telling him everything that had happened to her. And when at last the time came for him to go, and he asked, as he had so often asked before, "Beauty, will you marry me?"

She answered softly, "Yes, dear Beast."

As she spoke, a blaze of light sprang up before the windows of the palace; fireworks crackled and guns banged, and across the avenue of orange trees, in letters all made of fire-flies, was written: "Long live the Prince and his Bride!"

Turning to ask the Beast what it could all mean, Beauty found that he had disappeared and in his place stood her long-loved Prince! At the same moment, the wheels of a carriage were heard upon the terrace, and two ladies entered the room. One of them Beauty recognised as the stately lady who she had seen in her dreams; the other was also so grand and queenly that Beauty hardly knew which one to greet first.

But the one she already knew said to her companion, "Well, Queen, this is Beauty, who has had the courage to rescue your son from the terrible enchantment. They love one another, and only your consent to their marriage is needed in order to make them perfectly happy."

"I consent with all my heart," cried the Queen. "How can I ever thank you enough, charming girl, for having restored my dear son to his natural form?"

And then she tenderly embraced Beauty and the Prince, who had meanwhile been greeting the Fairy and receiving her congratulations.

"Now," said the Fairy to Beauty, "I suppose that you would like me to send for all your brothers and sisters to dance at your wedding?"

And so she did, and the marriage was celebrated the very next day with the utmost splendour, and Beauty and the Prince lived happily ever after.

CPSIA information can be obtained at www.ICGtesting.com
Printed in the USA
BVIW12n1947210417
481061BV00027B/138